MINI CLASSICS
BEAUTY
AND THE
BEAST

RETOLD BY STEPHANIE LASLETT
ILLUSTRATED BY ALISON WINFIELD

・PARRAGON・

TITLES IN SERIES I AND III OF THE MINI CLASSICS INCLUDE:

SERIES III

A PARRAGON BOOK

Published by
Parragon Books,
Unit 13–17, Avonbridge Trading Estate,
Atlantic Road, Avonmouth, Bristol BS11 9QD

Produced by
The Templar Company plc,
Pippbrook Mill, London Road, Dorking, Surrey RH4 1JE

Designed by Mark Kingsley-Monks

Printed and bound in Great Britain

ISBN 1-85813-704-7

Long ago there lived a wealthy merchant. He was very rich and had many precious belongings but his greatest treasures were his three beautiful daughters. He loved them all but it was the youngest, a girl of tender kindness and fragile beauty, who was his favourite.

One day the merchant made ready to sail away on a voyage of trade. He sent for his daughters to ask what gifts they would like from the lands across the sea.

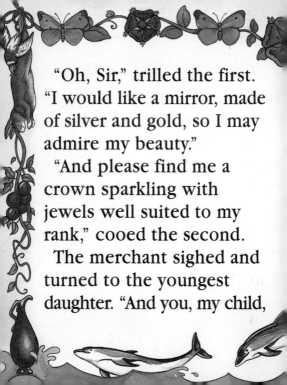

"Oh, Sir," trilled the first. "I would like a mirror, made of silver and gold, so I may admire my beauty."

"And please find me a crown sparkling with jewels well suited to my rank," cooed the second.

The merchant sighed and turned to the youngest daughter. "And you, my child, what is your desire?"

"A rose, dear father, to please my heart. Just a perfect rose of the darkest, truest red."

The merchant sailed away in a fine ship and for many months he traded with men from far-off lands. Some bowed and scraped and eyed his purse jealously.

Some stood, stony-faced
to drive a harder bargain,
then laughed and clapped
their hands on his to seal
the deal. The merchant
travelled long and far. He
bartered carpets for canvas
and silks for spices, wine
for wood and cotton for
carvings — and all the while
his wealth increased.

His business done, he sought to buy the promised gifts. He soon found a mirror, all silver and gold, and a well-bred crown, sparkling with bright jewels, but a perfect rose of darkest red? Where should he look? In the gardens of kings he saw many fine blooms, but none was quite perfect.

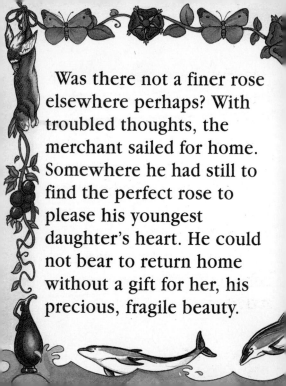

Was there not a finer rose elsewhere perhaps? With troubled thoughts, the merchant sailed for home. Somewhere he had still to find the perfect rose to please his youngest daughter's heart. He could not bear to return home without a gift for her, his precious, fragile beauty.

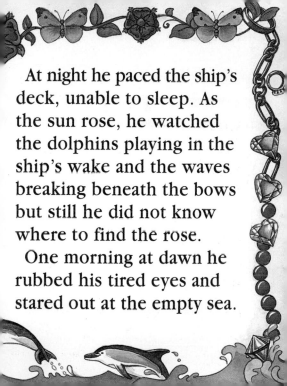

At night he paced the ship's deck, unable to sleep. As the sun rose, he watched the dolphins playing in the ship's wake and the waves breaking beneath the bows but still he did not know where to find the rose.

One morning at dawn he rubbed his tired eyes and stared out at the empty sea.

Suddenly a pirate ship appeared as if from nowhere. The merchant sprang to turn his ship around and make for safety, but it was not to be.

18

The wind was in the brigands' favour and in no time they were close by. To the merchant's horror, they leapt aboard with snarling faces and sharp cutlasses. They took his boat and all his gold and goods, then laughing cruelly, cast him overboard into the deep and rolling sea.

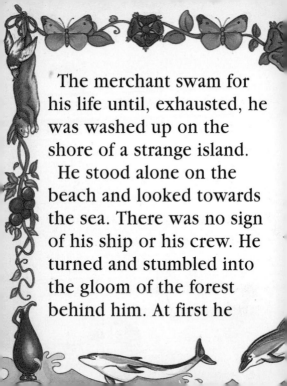

The merchant swam for
his life until, exhausted, he
was washed up on the
shore of a strange island.
He stood alone on the
beach and looked towards
the sea. There was no sign
of his ship or his crew. He
turned and stumbled into
the gloom of the forest
behind him. At first he

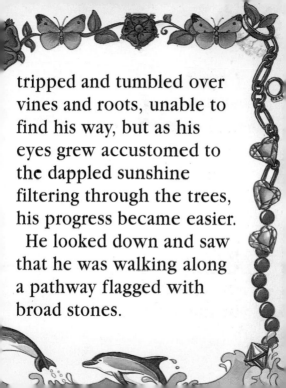

tripped and tumbled over
vines and roots, unable to
find his way, but as his
eyes grew accustomed to
the dappled sunshine
filtering through the trees,
his progress became easier.

He looked down and saw
that he was walking along
a pathway flagged with
broad stones.

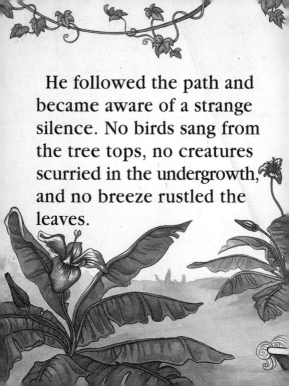

He followed the path and became aware of a strange silence. No birds sang from the tree tops, no creatures scurried in the undergrowth, and no breeze rustled the leaves.

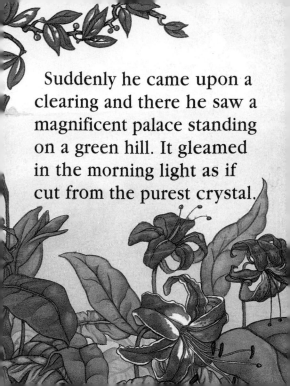

Suddenly he came upon a clearing and there he saw a magnificent palace standing on a green hill. It gleamed in the morning light as if cut from the purest crystal.

As the merchant drew near to the palace, the eerie silence of the forest gave way to the faint sound of sweet music. He could see that the palace windows and the great arched gateway were thrown wide open.

There was no-one to be seen so he walked through the gate into a beautiful garden. It was filled with exotic flowers of every shape and colour. Trees laden with fruit dipped down, kissing their reflections in crystal-clear pools that darted with golden fishes.

Inside the palace elegant furniture stood in the hallways and fine carpets lay on the polished floors.

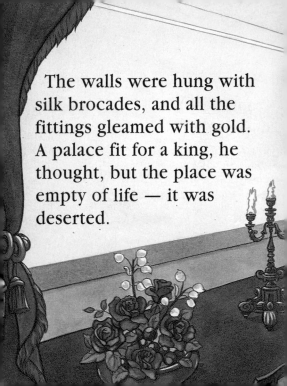

The walls were hung with silk brocades, and all the fittings gleamed with gold. A palace fit for a king, he thought, but the place was empty of life — it was deserted.

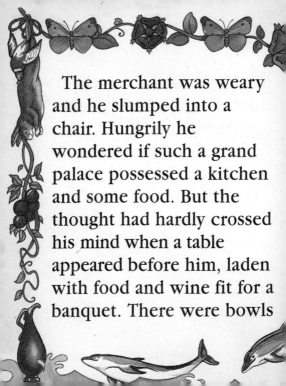

The merchant was weary and he slumped into a chair. Hungrily he wondered if such a grand palace possessed a kitchen and some food. But the thought had hardly crossed his mind when a table appeared before him, laden with food and wine fit for a banquet. There were bowls of plump and juicy fruit, sides of beef and ham, nuts and crusty bread, and flagons of spring water and ruby wine.

The merchant ate his fill and tipping back the last tankard of wine, he yawned. He was almost asleep on his feet as he slowly climbed the staircase.

Finding a bedchamber to his liking, he kicked off his boots and stretched out on the great, soft bed. In no time at all he was fast asleep and snoring loudly.

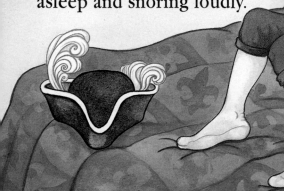

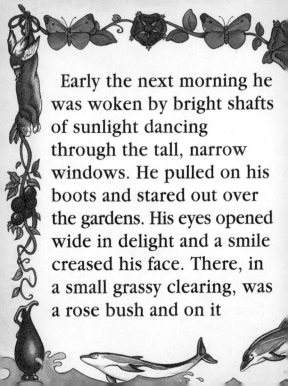

Early the next morning he was woken by bright shafts of sunlight dancing through the tall, narrow windows. He pulled on his boots and stared out over the gardens. His eyes opened wide in delight and a smile creased his face. There, in a small grassy clearing, was a rose bush and on it

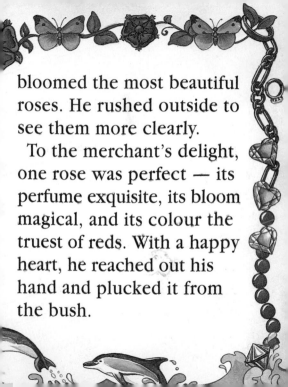

bloomed the most beautiful roses. He rushed outside to see them more clearly.

To the merchant's delight, one rose was perfect — its perfume exquisite, its bloom magical, and its colour the truest of reds. With a happy heart, he reached out his hand and plucked it from the bush.

At last he had found the rose to please his youngest daughter's heart.

But as soon as he picked the beautiful flower, the sky blackened, lightning flashed and a crack of thunder split the angry sky. Then from behind him came a terrifying roar that shook the earth beneath his feet.

The merchant spun round
in terror. Towering over
him he saw a terrible being,
neither man nor animal —
a raging, ugly Beast!

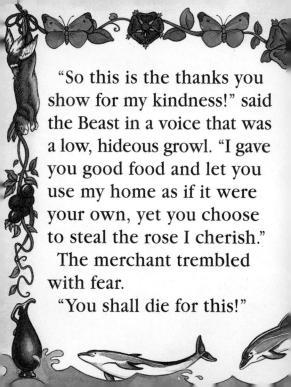

"So this is the thanks you show for my kindness!" said the Beast in a voice that was a low, hideous growl. "I gave you good food and let you use my home as if it were your own, yet you choose to steal the rose I cherish."

The merchant trembled with fear.

"You shall die for this!"

raged the Beast.

"But the rose was not for me," stammered the terrified merchant. "It was for my child, the sweetest of my daughters."

The Beast drew back, his twisted brows clenched in thought.

"So be it. You must let your child take your place.

Let her come here of her own free will and I will let you live." So saying, the Beast reached into a pocket with one huge paw and dropped a golden ring into the merchant's hand.

"Take this ring and guard it carefully. Within three days she must be here or you will die!"

43

The merchant stared down at the ring in dismay. How could he let his lovely daughter take his place here with this terrible creature? But when he looked up the Beast had vanished and to his amazement he found himself in his own home with the rose and the ring still clasped in his hands.

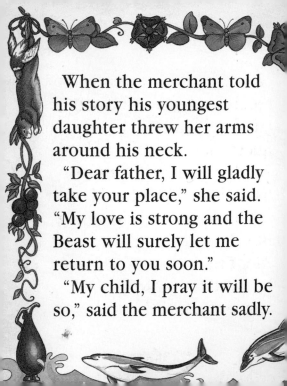

When the merchant told his story his youngest daughter threw her arms around his neck.

"Dear father, I will gladly take your place," she said. "My love is strong and the Beast will surely let me return to you soon."

"My child, I pray it will be so," said the merchant sadly.

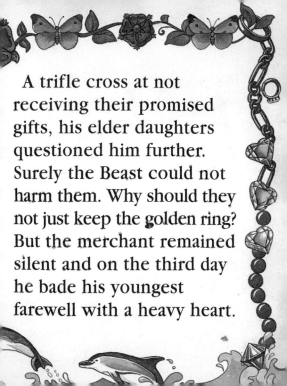

A trifle cross at not receiving their promised gifts, his elder daughters questioned him further. Surely the Beast could not harm them. Why should they not just keep the golden ring? But the merchant remained silent and on the third day he bade his youngest farewell with a heavy heart.

His favourite daughter
took up the rose and
slipped the ring on her
finger. In a flash she found
herself standing by the
rose bush in the enchanted
garden. The rose lifted
from her hand and bound
itself to the severed stem
where it bloomed even
brighter than before.

The music that played
through the trees and the
scent of the flowers filled
her with delight. Soon she
came upon the beautiful
palace and walking through
the great doorway she
marvelled at the beautiful
things in the many fine
rooms and felt quite at ease
and unafraid.

When dusk fell she went
into the great hall to dine.
Somehow it was no
surprise to see the table set
with dishes of delicate
flavour, served in the finest
crystal and porcelain.

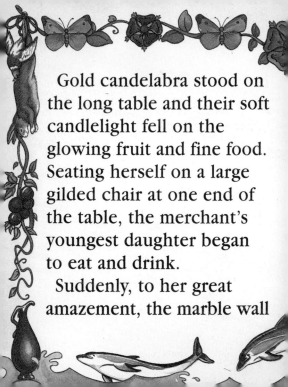

Gold candelabra stood on the long table and their soft candlelight fell on the glowing fruit and fine food. Seating herself on a large gilded chair at one end of the table, the merchant's youngest daughter began to eat and drink.

Suddenly, to her great amazement, the marble wall

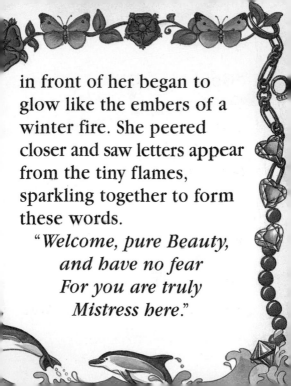

in front of her began to glow like the embers of a winter fire. She peered closer and saw letters appear from the tiny flames, sparkling together to form these words.

"Welcome, pure Beauty,
and have no fear
For you are truly
Mistress here."

No sooner had she read
the message than the
flames disappeared. Beauty
looked around her but to
her disappointment there
was no one in sight and
the great palace was silent.

Each day the merchant's youngest daughter awoke to a new delight: the finest silk gowns were laid out for her choice; the finest food was always to her taste; and the gardens sang with soft music. The sweet-scented blooms parted before her and their fragrance filled the balmy air.

At the end of the day when she felt tired, her feet were lifted and she was carried along as if on a summer's breeze. And so it was that Beauty felt well cared for.

Day followed day and she grew fond of her unseen master. It was clear that he loved her dearly. Each evening she read the fiery

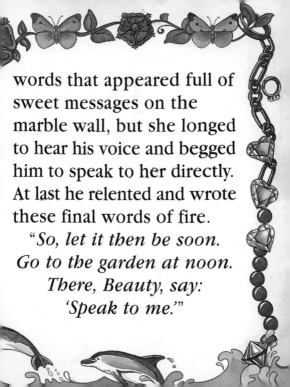

words that appeared full of sweet messages on the marble wall, but she longed to hear his voice and begged him to speak to her directly. At last he relented and wrote these final words of fire.

"So, let it then be soon.
Go to the garden at noon.
There, Beauty, say:
'Speak to me.'"

The following day she went to the garden well before noon. She was so excited at the thought of hearing her master's voice that she laughed and skipped as she ran towards the sun-dial.

There she waited patiently until at last the sun was high overhead. Then quietly she said, "Speak to me."

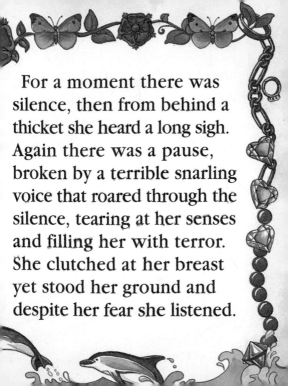

For a moment there was silence, then from behind a thicket she heard a long sigh. Again there was a pause, broken by a terrible snarling voice that roared through the silence, tearing at her senses and filling her with terror. She clutched at her breast yet stood her ground and despite her fear she listened.

At length she heard just words of kindness and no longer noticed the fearsome voice which spoke them. Her fear vanished and from that moment the Beast and the Beauty spoke each day.

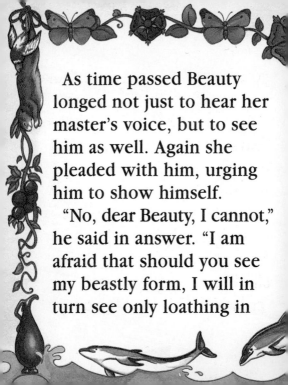

As time passed Beauty longed not just to hear her master's voice, but to see him as well. Again she pleaded with him, urging him to show himself.

"No, dear Beauty, I cannot," he said in answer. "I am afraid that should you see my beastly form, I will in turn see only loathing in your eyes and that I could not bear."

She began to cry and her tears softened his heart so much that at last he agreed to grant her wish.

"Come to the garden at dusk when the shadows are at their deepest. Then say 'Show yourself, dear friend,' and I will do so."

At dusk she said the chosen
words. A movement close
at hand caused her to turn.
For a fleeting second the
Beast was revealed, and in
that instant she saw a
creature so terrible that
she cried out in alarm and
fell senseless to the ground.
Some minutes passed but
at last she opened her eyes.

Then she saw the Beast
sitting among the beautiful
flowers of his garden with
his back toward her. To her
dismay she saw that his
shoulders shook with
dreadful sobs as he wept
bitterly. Suddenly she no
longer felt afraid. She walked
towards him and rested her
hand on his head.

The Beast raised his great
face towards her and his
cheeks were wet with tears.
Her kind heart was filled
with sorrow, for Beauty
knew that it was she who
had caused him such pain.

"Do not cry," she whispered. "I do not fear your form. It is only the shell that cloaks a tender heart. The wisdom that lies within is good and true. Please forgive me for hurting you so."

So saying, she took her lace
handkerchief and gently
wiped a tear from his cheek.
At her touch the terrible
face creased in a smile. From
that day they became loving
friends and, delighting in
each other's company,
shared the beauty of the
island — the ugly Beast
and the delicate Beauty.

One night the merchant's daughter slept fitfully. She tossed and turned on her bed and woke with a start from a terrible dream. She cried out and the Beast rushed to her side.

Her dream had been of her dear father, sick in his bed and close to death. The Beast tried to comfort her, but his kind heart knew that she would not rest until she stood by her father's side. He bade her return to her home.

"Go now, Beauty," he said kindly, "but remember, you

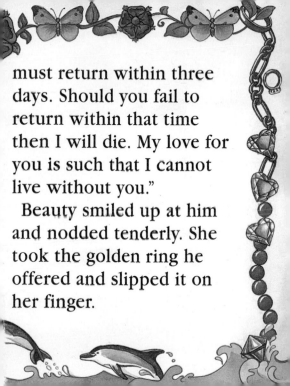

must return within three days. Should you fail to return within that time then I will die. My love for you is such that I cannot live without you."

Beauty smiled up at him and nodded tenderly. She took the golden ring he offered and slipped it on her finger.

Her father was so pleased
to see his beloved daughter
that within a couple of days
he was dancing about in
the best of health. She told
him her story and told of
her love for the Beast. Her
eldest sister snorted and
the second sister scowled
and said, "If he is so ugly,
does he not deserve to die?"

"Dear sister," replied Beauty. "That is an unworthy thought. I could not be so cruel to so kind and gentle a being."

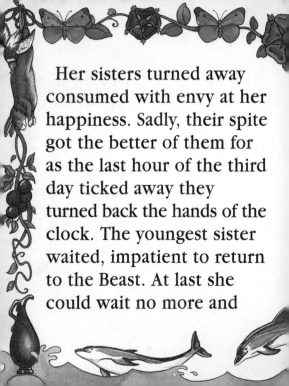

Her sisters turned away consumed with envy at her happiness. Sadly, their spite got the better of them for as the last hour of the third day ticked away they turned back the hands of the clock. The youngest sister waited, impatient to return to the Beast. At last she could wait no more and

saying goodbye, slipped the ring on her finger and vanished — back to the enchanted palace.

But the palace was silent; no birds sang in the still gardens and no gentle music played through the fine chambers. Frantically she searched for the Beast and at last she found him.

He lay still on the ground and clutched to his breast was the single, dark red rose. Its petals had fallen and she knew at once that he was dead.

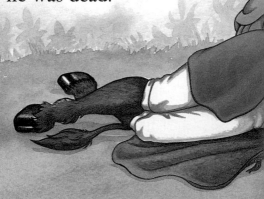

She knelt beside him and rested her hand on his twisted brow. She felt the tears well in her eyes and bent slowly to kiss his cheek. A single tear fell onto the Beast's heart as her eyes filled with the pain of sorrow and the daylight suddenly clouded from sunlight to dusk. Falling, she gave up her senses and slumped over the dead body of the Beast and knew no more.

Her eyes opened in surprise to the chatter of a hundred voices. She was sitting on a silver throne and standing beside her was a handsome prince. He smiled kindly down at her.

The hall before her was full of noblemen and their ladies. Among them she saw her father, his hands clasped together and beaming broadly. Her two sisters stood beside him, shame-faced. Beauty moved down the steps towards them but the prince took her hand and spoke softly.

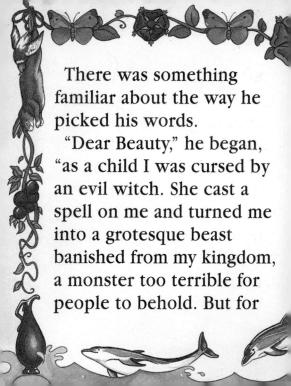

There was something familiar about the way he picked his words.

"Dear Beauty," he began, "as a child I was cursed by an evil witch. She cast a spell on me and turned me into a grotesque beast banished from my kingdom, a monster too terrible for people to behold. But for

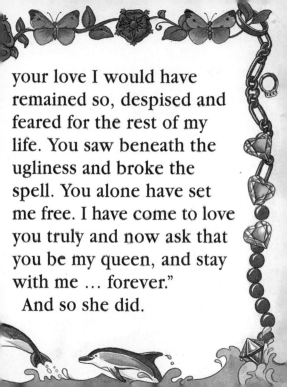

your love I would have remained so, despised and feared for the rest of my life. You saw beneath the ugliness and broke the spell. You alone have set me free. I have come to love you truly and now ask that you be my queen, and stay with me ... forever."

And so she did.

MADAME DE VILLENEUVE

The Beauty and the Beast was first written by
Madame de Villeneuve and published in 1740.
A long and rather dull tale, it was rewritten by
Madame de Beaumont in 1756 and translated
into English the following year.
The main theme of the story is seen again and
again in many tales worldwide; the girl (or
sometimes boy) who has to marry an animal
which later, through the strength of their love,
is transformed into a human.
Madame de Beaumont's version proved
immediately popular. She wrote it whilst
working as a governess in England and evidently
hoped that the story's moral message would be
an important lesson for her young charges.